Dubs Runs for President

Written by

Dick Morris
Eileen McGann and
Clayton J. Liotta

Illustrated by

Clayton J. Liotta

Dubs Runs for President

Requests for permission to make copies of any part of the work should be submitted online at info@velocity-press.com or mailed to Velocity Press, Suite 1000, 49 Twin Lakes Road, South Salem, NY 10590.

Library of Congress Cataloging-in-Publication Data is pending.

Printed in the United States of America

ISBN-13: 978-1-938804-03-8
ISBN-10: 1-938804-03-1

www.velocity-press.com

Velocity Press

When Dubs came home from Washington, he was feeling so tired
That a nice, long nap was all he desired.

When he closed his eyes, he began to dream
Of all the wonders that he had seen.

The monuments and statues of our presidents past
And how they built this great country that grew so fast.

When Dubs awoke he no longer felt tired,
In fact, he was actually downright inspired.

Could I become a famous leader just like them?
Of dogs and cats and women and men?

Can I do something dogs don't usually do?
Run for president of this great country, too?

Dubs called over his old friend Daisy

And said "I want to run for president, do you think I'm crazy?

I want to help my country and be the first dog elected

And, Daisy, you're the vice president I have selected.

I can promise that I'll give it my best, my all,

But I still want to play with my tennis ball."

"Dubs for president?" wondered the newspapers and TV,
The first dog candidate that they ever did see,

And when Dubs announced that he was really going to run,
Reporters came running from everywhere under the sun.

Word got around and in a matter of days,
People were talking about Dubs, the latest craze.

Everywhere Dubs and Daisy went they saw
That all the crowd wanted was to shake his paw.

To run for president, if you want to win,
It's hard to figure out where to begin.

So Daisy told Dubs, "Before this race is over
May I recommend you hire Mr. Karl Rover.

Karl knows the ins and outs. He knows the ropes
And he'll help us achieve our fondest hopes."

"You've become overnight a big sensation,
But to win," Karl said, "you must get the nomination.

Let's get to work, we have little time,
To win the nomination of the Party K-9."

Iowa was the first state to vote,

and Dubs visited every farm, no matter how remote.

With each hand he shook and baby he licked,

He became sure that he would be picked.

When the votes came in, Dubs won the state

And now his campaign really started to rate.

New Hampshire was the next state on the list,

So they drove all night through the rain and the mist.

Although the campaign bus was comfy inside,

Dubs preferred to run alongside.

And once again, he worked his magic,

To lose now would just be tragic,

Because people had begun really to heed,

His message that a dog president was just what we need.

But there were other dogs who wanted to run,
They felt being president would be such fun.

So they met in the K-9 Party debate
To see who would be the candidate.

But the poodle only doodled,
While the other dog just barked.

So when Dubs told all about his trip to D.C.,
Everyone realized what a great president he would be.

The other party did not want Dubs to win,

So their own campaign they did formally begin.

Felix the Cat was pretty and fine,

So he got the nomination of the Party Feline.

Dubs sat down for his interview on TV,
Calm and confident and strong as can be.

Then to scratch an itch he rolled on his back,
And old Karl Rover blew his stack.

"You've got to sit still in an interview like that,
Otherwise you'll lose the election to that silly cat."

Dubs promised to fight America's worst enemies,
To deal with them Dubs had the perfect remedies.

Fido Castro, Vladimir Poodle, and Hugo Chihuahua better beware,
Because Dubs was prepared to go right over there.

All the nation's dogs stayed up very late
To watch the K-9 Party choose its final candidate.

Dubs appeared in the huge convention hall
And spoke at great length of his promises for all.

"I pledge," he said, "to give one and all
Your very own yellow tennis ball.

And dogs should be allowed," Dubs then said,
"To sleep with their owners right on the bed."

So Dubs faced Felix in the general election,
One would win, the other face rejection.

They each worked hard to get every last vote,
Campaigning by car, air, train, and boat.

Dubs was out every day, sun or rain,
Traveling around our nation in his own private train.

And every time that train came to a stop,
Dubs gave a speech and came out on top.

A horse named Gallop took a poll
To see which of the candidates was on a roll.

Dubs was ahead of Felix, that much was clear,
His victory, he realized, was definitely quite near.

While watching Wolf News they saw something unexpected.

Dubs got the most votes, he was elected!

America was so happy, there was a big celebration.

Now Dubs would be president of the world's greatest nation.

And everyone could finally see

Just how wonderful democracy can be.

But Dubs started to get scared.

Can I do the job? Would I know how?

Would I say bow when the nation needed a wow?

Being president is a full-time call,

Would I have to give up my beloved tennis ball?

This is quite serious, it is no joke

But then with a start Dubs awoke.

No matter how real it often did seem,

His candidacy had actually been only a dream.

I love my country but I'm really quite lucky
That I'm not the president, I'm just a puppy.

But visiting Washington had been such fun
That Dubs wanted to see where it had all begun.

So Dubs said to Daisy, "Don't be astounded,
I want to go back to where our country was founded,

To Philadelphia, the original capital site,
Where America first got this democracy thing right."

And so it was on to Philadelphia for the furry pair,
To see the history that was waiting there....

COLOR ME

Don't forget to draw in my tennis ball!

COLOR ME

Where would you hide my tennis ball?